Bert's Band

Retold by Martin Waddell
Illustrated by Tim Archbold

Collins

Bert had a brass band and they played:
OOMPAH-BANG-BANG-TING-A-LING!

3

Bert's Band won the Band Cup. They played:
OOMPAH-BANG-BANG-TING-A-LING!

They played all the way home on the bus.
OOMPAH-BANG-BANG-TING-A-LING!

They got off the bus at midnight.

Bert told his band, "Take off your socks and your boots."

The band asked, "What for?"

Bert said, "So we won't wake anyone up!"

They took off their socks and their boots.

Bert said, "Shhhhh! Go on tippy-toes!"

So ... Bert's Band tip-toed up the main street playing:
OOMPAH-BANG-BANG-TING-A-LING!

13

Come to hear

Bert's Band

Every Saturday,
2pm at the
park bandstand

Winners of the Band Cup!

✿ Ideas for guided reading ✿

Learning objectives: moving through the text attending to meaning, etc; discussing content of text; describing incidents from their own experience in an audible voice; reciting stories and rhymes with predictable and repeating patterns, also extending and inventing; blending phonemes to read CVC words; interpreting a text by reading aloud with pace and emphasis; interpret a text by reading aloud with pace and emphasis.

Curriculum links: Science: Sounds and Hearing; Citizenship: Taking Part

High frequency words: had, a, and, they, the, all, way, on, his, off, your, what, for, said, so, we, took, their, go

Interest words: brass, won, home, midnight, told, socks, boots, anyone, shhhhh!, tippy-toes

Word count: 117

Resources: Whiteboard and pens

Getting started

- Look at the front cover and read the title together.

Ask the children to tell you what a band is and what type of instruments a band might play. List all the instruments on a whiteboard.

- Read pp2–3 together. Practise reading *'OOMPAH-BANG-BANG-TING-A-LING!'* together, saying it loudly, quietly and rhythmically.

- Walk through the book with the children, looking at the pictures and discussing what is happening.

- Ask them to practise blending all three phonemes in CVC words, for example *had, cup, bus*.

Reading and responding

- Ask children to read the story aloud and independently up to p13, and observe, prompt and praise attempts to read challenging words. Discuss what they can do if they get stuck on a word, for example look at the pictures, use awareness of the grammar (sense) of the sentence.

- Praise children for using expression when reading *'OOMPAH-BANG-BANG-TING-A-LING!'*.

- Using pp14–15, ask the children what the band is doing in this picture. Read the poster together and

i

Mentoring for
Doctors and Dentists

Mentoring in Medicine

by

Dr Romesh Gupta, MD FRCP FRCP(E) MBA
Honorary Senior Lecturer in Medical Education,
Postgraduate School of Medicine and Health,
University of Central Lancashire, Preston.
Consultant Physician,
Chorley and South Ribble District General Hospital,
Preston Road,Chorley, Lancs PR7 1PP, UK

and

Professor Sundara (Sam) Lingam, MD (Hons) FRCPCH FRCPS DCH DRCOG
Professor of Medical Education,
Saba University School of Medicine, Antelles, The Netherlands.
Consultant Paediatrician in Community Child Health,
St Ann's Hospital, Tottenham, London N15 3TH, UK

© 2000 by
Blackwell Science Ltd

Editorial Offices:
Osney Mead, Oxford OX2 0EL
25 John Street, London WC1N 2BL
23 Ainslie Place, Edinburgh EH3 6AJ
350 Main Street, Malden, MA 02148 5018, USA
54 University Street, Carlton, Victoria 3053, Australia
10, rue Casimir Delavigne, 75006 Paris, France

Other Editorial Offices:
Blackwell Wissenschafts-Verlag GmbH
Kurfürstendamm 57, 10707 Berlin, Germany

Blackwell Science KK
MG Kodenmacho Building, 7–10 Kodenmacho Nihombashi,
Chuo-ku, Tokyo 104, Japan

First published 2000.

Printed and bound in Great Britain.
Designed and set by Em Quad.

The Blackwell Science logo is a trade mark of Blackwell
Science Ltd, registered at the United Kingdom Trade Marks
Registry

DISTRIBUTORS
Marston Book Services Ltd
PO Box 269
Abingdon
Oxon OX14 4YN
orders:
Tel: 01235 465500
Fax: 01235 465555

USA
Blackwell Science, Inc.
Commerce Place
350 Main Street,
Malden, MA 02148 5018
orders:
Tel: 800 759 6012
     781-388-8250
Fax: 781-388-8255

Canada
Login Brothers Book Company
324 Saulteaux Crescent
Winnipeg, Manitoba R3J 3T2
Canada, L4W 4P7
orders:
Tel: 204-837-2987

Australia
Blackwell Science Pty Ltd
54 University Street
Carlton, Victoria 3053
orders:
Tel: 3-9347-0300
Fax: 3-9347-5001

A catalogue record for this title is available from the British
Library

ISBN: 0 632 05676 2

For further information on Blackwell Science, visit our
website:
www.blackwell-science.com

CONTENTS

"an experienced and trusted advisor".

HISTORY

Mentoring is a Greek word based on the story of Telemachus, the son of Odysseus and Penelope, who decided to seek out his father who had failed to return from the Trojan war. Telemachus's friend and advisor, named Mentor, offered to accompany him on his search. With the help of Mentor, Telemachus found his father and returned to Greece. He then discovered that Pallas Athene, the personification of wisdom, had assumed the shape of Mentor, who was too old to travel from Ithaca to Troy. It was she who had been Telemachus's mentor in his search for his father.

FOREWORD

Continuing professional development requires understanding of the principles of life-long learning. Part of this is recognition of the need to be able to help and seek the help of colleagues and to be listened to and aided in a similar manner. This is the basis behind mentoring.

This book gives a clear explanation of mentoring in action. It provides a system whereby an individual, who is usually more senior or experienced, can guide and support somebody more junior in their professional development.

As such, it is valuable and welcome. It particularly emphasizes that mentoring relationships are clear and that there is a two-way basis to them. Developing good mentoring practice for doctors is welcome and is now becoming an accepted part of good professional practice.

Professor John G Temple
Chair – COPMeD
August 1999

PREFACE

As we enter the new millennium the emphasis of medical practice is changing to ensure the provision of high quality evidence-based care to all patients throughout the UK. The Government's initiative of clinical governance seeks to raise the standard of professional competence by introducing regular appraisals and assessments, with the introduction of revalidation.

The Overseas Doctors' Association in the UK (ODA) looks forward to increasing its partnership activities throughout the medical profession and is also prepared to work across boundaries, seeking to benefit from the expertise already developed in other Government departments and in wider public and private sector organizations. If we are able to achieve this we will be able to set higher standards in both primary and specialist patient care in the UK.

Mentoring, career counselling, appraisal and assessments are some of the well recognized tools that are useful for professional development.

Bill Gormley with Dr Gupta and Professor Lingam: planning the mentoring training day.

While mentoring was initially introduced for the benefit of younger, less experienced trainee doctors, experience has shown that more senior practitioners have also gained from mentoring through their peers. This will help to establish a culture of openness where the sharing of good practice will facilitate early identification of knowledge and skill gaps in individual learning.

We feel that this publication will provide readers with some background information on the principles of mentoring. This will enable participants to maximize the benefits from the mentoring process.

Finally, we would like to thank Bill Gormley, Director of Human Resources of the Department of Social Security and his team for their contribution, guidance and support in developing the mentoring programme for doctors and dentists in the UK and also for their help in producing this publication.

Dr Romesh C Gupta   **Professor Sundara Lingam**

January 2000

The Overseas Doctors' Association (ODA) was formed on 11th May 1975 with the major aim of protecting and promoting the interests of doctors from overseas or of overseas origin who are working in the UK. There are about 23,000 overseas doctors working in the National Health Service (NHS), which is about 27 per cent of medical manpower. Around 1,500-2,000 overseas doctors enter the UK each year.

The Hospital Doctors' Forum of the ODA was set up to target overseas hospital doctors employed within the NHS. Its aim is to develop and promote effective health care in hospitals in the UK, taking into account the specific needs of ethnic minority communities.

The Forum is committed to the principle of continued life-long learning, professional development and training. We believe that mentoring is a useful development tool designed to encourage doctors to realize their full potential. This booklet on mentoring is one step to promote togetherness among doctors of ethnic minority origin.

The ODA also recognizes the need for training in appraisals and assessments which will become part of the new Professional Linguistic Assessment Board (PLAB) test for overseas doctors. All new overseas doctors in the NHS will be assessed by appraisal during their first post in the UK before getting full registration. Every doctor in the UK will also be subject to annual appraisal. In the year 2000 the ODA has plans to train its members in this important subject, and the second volume in this series will cover Appraisals and Assessment in Medicine.

Overseas doctors account for about one-third of doctors in the UK. The immigration rules and means of obtaining registration with the General Medical Council (GMC) will be included in the third volume of the series, which will deal with the PLAB examination, careers in hospital medicine in the UK, and examinations and entry to the specialists' register after GMC registration. We believe that every consultant should be familiar with this in order to help their trainees with career progression, and that every trainee will benefit from having all the information available in one book.

Mentoring has gained widespread recognition in many public and private sector organizations at many levels and can be beneficial to all who participate. There is no overall right or wrong way to mentor. Although a mutual understanding of what a mentoring relationship is trying to achieve is fundamental, it can be tailored to suit individual needs.

In this book we aim to provide an understanding of what mentoring for doctors is all about and to set out some guidelines to help and assist with the role of both mentors and mentees. Our aim is also to provide training for those who wish to become involved in mentoring, and to set up a register of mentors.

We are very grateful for the help, advice and assistance provided by Bill Gormley and his team in the Information Technology Services Agency of the Department of Social Security and also to Dr Nimal Rajah, assistant regional secretary of the Hospital Doctors' Forum for their help in compiling this book. We trust it will benefit both trainees and trainers, and we would welcome your comments and criticisms for future editions.

Thanks are given to Dr Surendra Kumar, chairman of ODA, who has been very helpful and supportive to us in the compilation of this book.

Dr Romesh C Gupta
National Vice-Chairman
Overseas Doctors' Association
Director — ODA Mentoring
Scheme

Professor Sundara Lingam
Chairman
Hospital Doctors' Forum
Overseas Doctors' Association
Director — ODA Mentoring
Scheme

January 2000

1.1 INTRODUCTION

The word 'mentor' is as old as history and of Greek origin. It has its roots in the words **remember, think, counsel**.

This book is a resource for mentees and mentors. It will be useful to overseas doctors, particularly those in training grades and those who have recently arrived in the UK. Doctors in difficulties may also find the mentor scheme useful.

The book can be used in a number of ways including the following:-

As a **resource**: It gives a clear idea of how to prepare for mentoring, conduct mentoring sessions, and maintain a mentoring relationship.

For **reflection**: It is a resource to consult, particularly before a mentoring session or after a session to reflect about what has happened.

To **stimulate** development as a mentor: It provides a challenge and stimulus to reflect upon the role of mentors.

To **stimulate development** as a mentee: It may help in self-development of the mentee.

For **discussion**: As a focus for discussion with a mentee in a mentoring session and with other mentors in the network. It may also be provided for discussion with the educational supervisor (every trainee will have an educational supervisor who is usually the consultant under whom the trainee works).

To **read** selectively: The chapter is designed to be read in any way which is appropriate. Either from page to page or by the sections relevant at the time.

1.2 MENTORING

Mentoring is a process in which a more skilled or experienced person (mentor) serves as a role model and supports, guides, advises, teaches, encourages, counsels and befriends a less skilled or experienced person, or a person who is in need of help for the purpose of promoting their professional and/or personal development.

- Mentoring functions are carried out within the context of an ongoing supportive relationship between the mentor and mentee.

- It is confidential for both parties and can involve a written contract or agreement if considered useful by both parties.

- Mentoring should be both non-judgmental and entirely voluntary.

- A doctor experiencing a difficulty related to training, performance, or immigration issues may find a mentor helpful, but a mentor might not be the best person to discuss problems related to postgraduate examinations. Such difficulties are best discussed with a regional advisor in the speciality in which the doctor works, or with the university postgraduate clinical tutor, who will be based in the postgraduate medical education centre (PGMC) (now called the staff development and education centre or similar).

- Career-related matters may be also discussed with the mentor (career counselling).

Dr Romesh Gupta welcoming the delegates and introducing the mentoring training.

1.3 MENTORING IN ACTION
Have you been mentored?

Most people have been helped at some time in their lives by another person in a senior position who has taken an interest in their welfare, and enabled them to develop by sharing their own experiences and knowledge.

When you think back to someone in your past who has helped you in this way you may not have thought of that person as a mentor at the time, but you know that it was an important relationship and had a valuable influence on you.

As a starting point, consider the following questions:

- Who took an interest in your welfare and development at a time when you were taking on challenges, i.e. entering your medical training or taking up your first post as a doctor?

- Who was a useful role model in your medical school?

- Who helped you uncover and use your hidden talent or ability?

- Who helped you face and resolve a difficult situation in your personal and professional life?

> "It was my mentor who convinced me that I need to change the way I approach my problems and suggested ways to overcome them."
>
> A MENTEE

- Who challenged you to acquire a new vision and direction in your life?

- What was it about these people who helped you?

Consultants who are from overseas may reflect back — would you have preferred to have had a mentor when you first came to UK?

Do you think it would have helped you?

Everyone needs a mentor. Have you a mentor now?

Who do you ring (or confide in) if you need advice?

1.4 VARIETY AND VISION IN MENTORING

Mentoring relationships may be:

Open — able to focus on any topic

Closed — restricted discussion topics

Public — others know that the relationship exists

Bill Gormley
skilfully engaging
the doctors -
learning by
example.

Private — few know that the relationship exists

Formal — agreed appointments, venues and timings

Informal — casual, operating on a "pop-in any time" basis.

There is no blueprint for ideal mentoring, it can be a one-off intervention or a long relationship, part of an existing friendship or formal and highly structured.

Different mentoring approaches include peer mentoring — consultant to consultant, particularly in the case of problems related to performance or conduct procedures and mentoring within the trainee/trainer relationship. As a rule, however, the mentor should not be the educational supervisor, college tutor or the regional adviser of the mentee as they have to do the appraisal and assessments and be involved with RITA (review of in-service training assessment for specialist registrars).

"I came from an Asian subcontinent country – I shake my head when I say 'yes'. It was my mentor who explained to me that this can be confusing for British people."

A MENTEE

Common to all mentoring is that mentees come to view things in a new light. Mentoring is about change — both responding to change in the environment and promoting change in the mentee. The basis of change is a new vision of the possibilities.

It might be possible for the mentor to set a target for the mentee to achieve. It is also possible that mentors will come to view themselves and their own situation in a new light.

The following are considered to be key elements in the mentoring relationship:

- The mentee selects the mentor (a list of trained mentors is available. The ODA has a list of ODA trained consultants).

- A mentee can have more than one mentor.

- Each mentor develops different aspects of the mentee.

- Mentor and mentee must agree on the area for improvement.

- The mentor's concern is for the mentee, the hospital, trust or practice in which they work and the NHS as a whole.

- The mentee has potential for development.

- The mentee must be willing to learn and change.

- Being mentored is a challenging relationship as well as a supporting one. Constructive criticism can help the mentee face the need to change. The mentor has wider or different knowledge, experience and skills from the mentee and it is these skills which the mentor should use during a mentoring session.

- Each mentoring relationship has a natural life span. When one relationship ends, further learning will occur in new mentoring relationships.

- The ODA mentoring scheme may be the first experience the mentee has of being formally mentored. It may continue long after the initial contact with other mentors in the United Kingdom or overseas.

Mentees — keep in touch with mentors — send a Christmas card or New Year letter for example.

> "I used to smile and show my teeth when I speak — This can also be off- putting, said my mentor."
>
> **A MENTEE**

1.5 MENTORING IS ABOUT HELPING

Trainees would like consultant mentors to be frank and honest. They want the consultant to understand them but in return they will understand where the consultant is coming from.

Have a one-to-one — it will help.

> "Applying too much oil on the head is cultural but in the UK it is not necessary...Talking about how I behave helped me a lot."
>
> **A MENTEE.**

Dr Gupta in action

What can I do to help?

The ODA has a list of ODA consultants who have been trained in mentoring.

1.6 A THREE-STAGE MODEL OF MENTORING

Mentoring includes a number of processes. Different mentors have different strengths and work in different ways. Whatever the approach or style the mentor uses they usually find that a framework is of most help to the mentee. The three-stage model is as follows:-

I.   Exploration

II. New understanding

III. Action planning

"Mentoring gives me a real buzz and makes me feel unbelievably good that somebody can learn and develop with my help. It has enabled my influence to spread and thus assist the change process in a way which is more powerful than any other process I know."

AN EXPERIENCED MENTOR

How the model can be used:

- To reflect upon what mentoring involves, and to assess yourself as a mentor.

- As a schedule for a mentoring meeting — to work through stages.

- As a map of the mentoring process — to see what ground has been covered and what needs further attention.

- To reflect on the mentoring relationship over time as the mentee moves towards achieving the objectives they identified at the start of the relationship.

A mentor is in a position to model what one should or could **be** and not what one should or could **do**.

1.6.1 STAGE I — EXPLORATION

- Strategies you use:

  - take the lead
  - pay attention to the relationship and develop it
  - clarify the aims and objectives of mentoring
  - support and counsel.

- Methods you use:

  - listen
  - ask open questions
  - negotiate an agenda.

How to make the most of Stage I

Give it time and be patient. Action plans come unstuck when rushed. Insufficient exploration leads to faulty understanding in Stage II. Investment of time and care in Stage I pays dividends later in the meeting and the relationship.

Take the lead in creating a rapport with your mentee. Mentoring should take place in an atmosphere that encourages exploration. Help your mentee to arrive at his or her own answers.

Professor Lingam with one of the 'mentees' in a training session — practice makes perfect.

> *'I find it extremely useful to take brief notes and summarize the action to be taken at the end of each mentoring session. Opening up the next session with a review of the actions taken places some responsibility on the mentee to progress his/her situation.'*
>
> **AN EXPERIENCED MENTOR**

1.6.2 STAGE II — NEW UNDERSTANDING

- Strategies you use:

  - support and counsel
  - coach and demonstrate skills
  - offer constructive feedback

- Methods you use:

  - listen and challenge, ask both open and closed questions
  - recognize strengths and weaknesses
  - share experiences
  - establish priorities
  - identify developmental needs
  - give information and advice

How to make the most of Stage II

Stage II is the turning point in the process. New understanding releases energy. Once your mentee sees things differently, offer encouragement. Progress can be rapid, but again, do not rush.

Share stories from your own experience. It will help your mentee consolidate their learning. Do not share too soon.

Arriving at a new understanding might be uncomfortable - the mentee may be resistant. Be supportive and sensitive so that when you challenge, your mentee is able to learn.

1.6.3 STAGE III — ACTION PLANNING

- Strategies you use:

  - examine options for action and their consequences
  - attend to the mentoring process and the relationship
  - negotiate the action plan for the next meeting

- Methods you use:

  - encourage new and creative ways of thinking
  - help with decision-making and problem-solving
  - agree action plans
  - monitor progress and evaluate outcomes

How to make the most of Stage III

When stages I and II are done thoroughly, stage III is straight-forward and uses familiar management skills.

Plans are followed through when your mentee owns the solution. Give advice sparingly. Enhance commitment to change by using clear agreements and target setting.

Look after the relationship and discuss its progress with your mentee. Don't expect every meeting to end in an action plan. Sometimes the action will simply be to meet again, and that will be progress enough.

1.7 HOW DO YOU KNOW THAT YOU ARE READY TO BE A MENTOR?

Mentoring is a common, often unrecognized activity. It is a form of helping that most people develop further. Effective mentoring requires certain personal qualities and skills. Mentors need formal training on communication skills, the laws related to education and training (particularly involving the speciality in which the mentor is working), current immigration rules, GMC rules in relation to registration, performance procedures, self-regulation etc.

A mentor can address this in a number of ways:

- Recognizing and reflecting on the mentoring you have done already:

  - What do you do well?
  - What would you like to develop further?

- Reflecting upon your experience of being a mentee:

  - What did you value?
  - What did not help?

- Talking to other mentors:

  - What can you learn from them?
  - Would you emulate them?

- Talking to people you have mentored:

  - How do they rate you as a mentor?
  - Would they recommend you as a mentor?

- Pause for thoughts:

  - Consider the differences between mentoring and educational supervision. As a rule a good educational supervisor would not necessarily be a good mentor. Appreciate the overlap as well as the differences.
  - Consider the differences between mentoring and other ways of helping, e.g. teaching, counselling, appraisal and assessment.

> *"To be a successful mentor enjoy what you are doing as well as believe in your mentee. Do not hesitate to ask for help from other mentors with special expertise. It is important to be friends and have a rapport between people. The enriching experiences of meeting interesting people and facing the challenges of solving difficult problems are similar to the rewards of being a mentor. A good mentor therefore brings enjoyment of people and ideas and strong belief to the mentoring situation."*
>
> A CONSULTANT MENTOR WITH MANY YEARS EXPERIENCE.

ODA mentors receive structured training on rules and regulations, on basic and higher (Calman) specialist training, immigration rules, GMC performance procedures, assessment and appraisal, racial equality rules, etc.

You do not need to be from overseas to be an ODA-trained mentor.

1.8 CHARACTERISTICS OF A MENTOR
Are you a mentor?
You can also address this question by comparing yourself with the following list of characteristics of effective mentors.

Do you have:

- An experience of being a mentee?

- Relevant job-related experience and skills?

- Time? (Each mentee might need out-of-work time, minimum of one hour per week for a mentoring session.)

- Well developed inter-personal skills? (Training can be given.)

- An ability to relate well to people who want to learn? (Good teachers can be good mentors; most gurus are mentors.)

- A desire to help and develop mentees?

- An open mind, a flexible attitude and a recognition of your own need for support?

- Willingness to support a relationship with mentees?

It is a natural human impulse to help others, particularly if you know them. In a mentee/mentor relationship you need to help others about whom you may know very little. As an experienced and knowledgeable person you have something valuable to pass on. Mentoring is a natural way to influence others and the NHS for the good. If you have a desire to work with people in this way then you are ready to be a mentor.

NO-ONE FORGETS A GOOD MENTOR

PART 2

2.1 WHAT MENTORS DO

Mentors help mentees to:

- Establish themselves quickly in their learning and social environment.

- Gain knowledge and skills (particularly related to personal and social skills).

- Understand the working of the Royal Colleges, and their faculties, the NHS Trusts, British Medical Association (BMA), GMC, ODA etc.

- Develop personally.

- Acquire expertise in fields in which they need improvement.

- Understand appropriate behaviour in different situations.

- Understand different and conflicting ideas.

- Develop values and an ethical perspective.

- Adjust to change.

- Question their responses to certain issues, problems and situations.

- Overcome setbacks and obstacles.

- Acquire an open, flexible attitude to learning.

- Enjoy the challenges of change.

It is recommended that all trainees should join the BMA and those from overseas, or with overseas parentage, join the ODA. Encourage them to do so. Also mentors should ask the mentees to read the GMC documents **Good Medical Practice** and **Maintaining Good Medical Practice**.

> *"Mentors can give us a new language so that we can think differently and gain new perspectives."*
>
> **A MENTEE**

2.2 FINDING A MENTEE

Does the mentor find a mentee or does a mentee find a mentor? The answer is both. Mentoring relationships begin in all sorts of ways, both formal and informal. However they begin, it is important that the starting point is the mentee's needs and aspirations.

In the ODA scheme, your mentee may be somebody you know already or you may ask to be paired with someone new. The ODA will assist in identifying a suitable mentor/mentee partnership.

What would you like them to know about you? Put yourself in their position. The information you give about yourself needs careful thought.

2.3 BEING A MENTEE

People learn how to be a mentee through being part of a mentoring relationship. With experience and practice you will become better at making the most of the mentoring process.

Successful mentees accept challenges willingly. They are committed to the mentoring process.

Mentees must be willing to be active in their development and to see learning as a continuing process. When the mentee owns the process the quality of learning is improved, and this is a clinical governance issue for all doctors. Active mentees make progress faster and will become better doctors.

The mentor will help you to 'develop under your own power'. The mentee will be more willing to take risks when an atmosphere of mutual trust and respect exists. This is achieved through open discussion and regular contact.

What mentees can expect:
Mentees expect to:

- be challenged
- be coached
- develop greater self-confidence
- be supported and encouraged
- be assisted in developing their careers
- become more self-aware

- receive wise counsel

- gain friendship

- share critical knowledge

- listen and be listened to

- learn how the organization works

- learn from example

- learn from mistakes.

What mentees look for in their mentor:

- a sounding board

- a confidant

- a giver of encouragement

- a source of knowledge

- a constructively critical friend;

- access to organizational support

- access to emotional support networks.

Not everyone is naturally a good mentor, just as not everyone is naturally a good teacher — but these skills can be learned and developed with training.

2.4 QUESTIONS YOU MIGHT ASK YOUR MENTEE

"Tell me about your experience of ....?"

"What do you think this means?"

"What is there to learn here?"

"What general lessons can be drawn from your reflection on your experience?"

"Can we develop any broad principles to work to?"

"How can you apply this understanding?"

"How can I help you do this?"

What mentees and mentors talk about

- the mentee's work-related issues

- the mentor's work-related issues

- time management

- special projects

- personal issues

- domestic issues

- the mentee's specific issues e.g. training, GMC registration, GMC performance review, immigration matters, conduct issues at work, awards, discrimination at work

Mentee and mentor often rehearse arguments/presentations for use elsewhere.

Mentors and mentees should ensure that the mentee's educational supervisor knows that mentoring is happening. It should be the responsibility of the mentee to inform his/her supervisor.

2.5 HOW TO GET HELP FROM THE MENTOR SCHEME
Key things to think about:
Preparation — it is helpful to have an agenda for each meeting. Reflect on the nature of mentoring, the process as well as the outcomes. Think about your commitment to using mentoring well and giving it adequate time.

Getting to know each other — give this enough time. It is the basis of trust and working together. Share experiences from your past.

Time — your relationship will change over time. Many mentees and mentors notice that discussion topics widen and deepen.

Difficulties — sometimes things may go wrong. Nothing can replace honest and open discussion about the relationship. Try to let others know about the existence of your mentoring relationship to avoid any misunderstanding or resentment. Keep the relationship under review.

Ground rules — establish ground rules. These will include:-

- **confidentiality** – this is essential. Agree between yourselves where the boundaries of the relationship are going to be.

- **time commitment** – how much? And how often?

- **location** – where are you going to meet?

- **recording meetings** – will you record your meeting, and if so how? A diary or log?

2.6 AND WHEN IT ENDS

This is the only certain event in the relationship. The relationship may end when the mentee has reached a stage when he/she no longer feels the need for regular contact. The mentee is confident and able to move on.

It is important to consider how it will end. If the relationship has been successful, there will be cause for celebration and a sense of loss. Attend to both.

You may agree to meet socially or less frequently or simply call a halt. Mentors would like annual feedback on progress of mentees.

The final discussion

Look back and review your mentoring relationship and what you value about it.

- What were your original goals, and were they achieved?

- Did your goals change? Did you discover new goals/aspirations?

- What problems did you have and how did you resolve them?

- Would you seek a mentoring relationship again?

- Inform the ODA about your mentoring experience, whether good or bad. Any ideas on improvements will always be welcomed.

These questions are useful for reviewing the mentoring process.

2.7 HOW DOES MENTORING WORK IN THE ODA?

If you would like a mentor or you would like to be a mentor, contact the ODA to express your interest. (An application form for mentors is found at the end of this chapter - photocopy the form, complete it and send to the ODA).

If you are looking for a mentor, the ODA has a list of doctors who are interested in mentoring and you may be able to find a mentor from the list. Most mentors are consultants, and they need not be from overseas to be an ODA mentor. Mentors will be available in all specialities and in all areas.

If you are a mentee, select a mentor (preferably someone easily accessible to where you live and work) and contact them directly.

Have an informal discussion with someone you know in the ODA. The chairperson or secretary of the division or a senior member will be able to recommend mentor(s) in your region who will be able to help you. (Name and address and contact details are found in the ODA diary which is issued to every member).

At ODA meetings you might find a senior member with whom you can discuss your needs and select a suggested mentor. It may be that the recommended mentor is also attending the meeting and so initial contact could be made immediately.

Dates and times of ODA regional meetings are available from ODA headquarters.

Your educational supervisor might know about the ODA mentor scheme already and will let you have the details.

Overseas doctors are encouraged to become ODA members — trainees pay £25.00 per annum, others pay £50.00 per annum. (You can get tax relief too!).

Welcome aboard.

USEFUL ADDRESSES

British Medical Association
BMA House,
Tavistock Square,
London WC1H 9JP
Tel: 0171 387 4499
Fax: 0171 383 6400

General Dental Council
37 Wimpole Street,
London W1M 8DQ
Tel: 0171 887 3800
Fax: 0171 224 3294

General Medical Council
178 Great Portland,
London W1N 6JE
Tel: 0171 580 7642
Fax: 0171 915 3641

Overseas Doctors' Association
ODA House
316A Buxton Road
Great Moor
Stockport
SK2 7DD
Tel: 0161 456 7828
Fax: 0161 482 4535

Mr Bill Gormley
Director of Human resources
Room PP36C
Peelpah Control Centre
Blackpool Industrial Estate
Drunel Way
Blackpool
FY4 5ES

Dr Romesh C Gupta
Director – ODA Mentor
Scheme,
Consultant Physician,
Chorley & South Ribble NHS
Trust,
Preston Road, Chorley, Lancs
PR7 1PP
Tel: 01257 245287
Fax: 01257 245045

**Professor Sam (Sundara)
Lingam**
Director – ODA Mentor
Scheme,
Consultant Paediatrician in
Community Child Health,
St Ann's Hospital, Tottenham,
London N15 3TH
Tel: 0181 442 6331
Fax: 0181 442 6116

Note: All postgraduate Medical Centres have details of local Deans

ACKNOWLEDGEMENTS

We are grateful for the support and encouragement received from Dr S Kumar, chairman of the Overseas Doctors' Association in the UK and the members of the Hospital Doctors' Forum of the ODA. Also, thank you to the medical practitioners who participated in our training seminars.

We would also like to thank Mr John Sellick for his photography work in this publication, and Susan Reid for editorial assistance.

In 2000/2001 the ODA is planning to introduce two more publications in this series:

- **Appraisals and Assessments**
- **Career Counselling**

APPLICATION FORM TO BECOME AN ODA-TRAINED MENTOR

Dr ☐   Mr☐   Mrs☐   Professor ☐   Other ☐ (please specify)

First name: ....   Surname: ....

Your address for correspondence: Your hospital/home address:

....

....

....

Postcode: ....   Postcode: ....

Telephone: ....   Telephone: ....

Fax: ....   Fax: ....

Email: ....   Email: ....

Your speciality: ....   Grade: ....

Year of qualification: ....   No of years on grade: ....

Are you from overseas or from an ethnic minority community? ....Yes ☐ No ☐

If Yes, which country or community? ....

Are you a member of ODA? .... Yes ☐ No ☐
(you need not be a member to be an ODA-trained mentor)

I wish to become a ODA-trained mentor,
please send me details of training courses. ....☐

I wish to become a member, please send application form. ....☐

I am aware my name is now kept on a computer database (Data Protection Act). ....☐

Signature: ....   Date: ....

Please send the completed form to: Chairman, Hospital Doctor's Forum, ODA House
316A Buxton Road, Great Moor, Stockport SK2 7DD

FOR PHOTOCOPYING USE ONLY — DO NOT TEAR OFF